The Book of
One Tree

The Book of
One Tree

Short Stories by
ANNETTE R. SCHOBER
(GRACE DEER)

ENTRADA BOOKS
A Division of Northland Publishing

*This book is dedicated to all
people of the earth, with special thanks
to Al, my partner, daughter Terra, and Daisy,
my four-legged guide.*

FIRST EDITION
ISBN 0-87358-539-9
Library of Congress Catalog Number: 91-45466

Printed in the United States of America

*Cover Design by David Jenney
Text Design by Carolyn Gibbs*

Cataloging-in-Publication Data
Schober, Annette R.
The book of One Tree / by Annette R. Schober. -- 1st ed.
96 p.
ISBN 0-87358-539-9 (softcover) : $9.95
1. Indians of North America--Fiction.   I. Title.
PS3569.C5233B6   1992
813'.54--dc20   91-45466
                                                          CIP

4-92 / 2.5M / 0398

Contents

Prologue

Lottie knew she would be having one more child. She paced the floor of the small, weathered cabin, once her childhood home, now home to Amos and herself and their three other children—the family called One Tree.

She stopped pacing when she saw Amos walk down the forested rise behind the cabin; she stood inside the open back door and watched him. A short, stocky, dark-haired man, he wore his raven-black hair pulled severely back from his face. He looks like a stranger sometimes, Lottie thought, dressed in worn jeans and plaid shirt like any one of the local white people.

Over his left shoulder hung the hindquarters of the deer he had shot that morning. Lottie recalled seeing deer hunters in the fall, driving out in their jeeps and parking by the side of the road throughout the hills; Amos drove no car, and the deer was only hunted so that they could eat for a little longer without using the paper they were given to buy food. Lottie knew it was money, but it was still paper not worthy of having tobacco scattered on the ground out of respect for the Spirit.

Amos stopped on the top of the hill. The evening light from behind silhouetted him as he laid the deer down and raised his hands to the sky. Lottie knew he could feel her there, watching. Amos bent over then and pulled some silvery hair from the deer's hide. Scraping a small circle free of pine needles and grass on the ground, he built a tiny fire. He then drew crumpled bills from his pockets and laid them gently on the flames. Lottie could smell burning hair where she stood now, outside the cabin's sagging back door.

When there was nothing but ashes left, Amos scooped them up in his broad, calloused hand and, holding them to his midsection, turned in stark profile against the purple-and-crimson sky. He looked like the mountain behind him then—Eagle Mountain that had always been the sacred heart of their land.

When Lottie saw him standing like that, a human reflection of the spirit of the mountain, she saw all of their people again: the ones who had climbed the mountain, the ones who had touched the mountain, the ones who had gone home to the mountain, the ones who had run away from the mountain. And the ones who had died a long way from the mountain.

Amos no longer looked like a stranger to her, and she ran out to help him scatter the ashes beneath the edge of the trees. Amos nodded to her as she came up beside him, and then he silently grinned and gave a knowing tug to the front of her long skirt, which was stretched tightly across her round belly. The sky darkened to deep purple as they cast the ashes into the nighttime wind. As the wind carried the ashes across the now-black peak of Eagle Mountain, the baby stirred.

Lottie felt the movement and thought of all her children. Where would they go when they were old enough to reach the mountain? Would the mountain still be there when they were ready to go?

I thought the world was ending,
And I thought my time was ebbing,
And I thought all life was flowing
To destruction.

I ran out on the desert,
And I climbed up on the mesa,
And I tried to touch the sky
And hold a god.

A numbness in my fingertips,
A wind that rattled all my bones,
A voice that shook the earth's great core
Thundered on alone.

I knew I was but the air in my lungs,
I knew I was but the mesa whistling wind,
I knew I was but the dark cloud
That shed a gentle rain.

Shed your skin that binds your bones,
Shed your lungs that bind your voice,
Shed your self that binds your soul,
Come home, Come home, Come home.

—An Old Indian Chant

Lottie

Lottie stands by her door and watches her youngest child, her son Bernard, cross the road. He turns left, scuffing through the dry, brown pine needles on his way to the bus stop. It is one-quarter mile down to the road at the edge of the clearing. Lottie thinks of it as "The Clearing" from the old days, when her people's village lay scattered in dwellings of twos and threes under the pines all around it.

Kind of like the children do now at the edge of the clearing, waiting for the school bus. In twos and threes they stand, bright red and yellow and blue sweatshirts on the boys, pink, orange, and green sweaters on the girls. Bernard usually stands alone; sometimes he is hard to see at a distance, in his earth-colored corduroy jacket. He insists on wearing that jacket, fall, winter, and spring, no matter the weather.

Lottie sees him now, not quite in the clearing. He is off the road a few yards, head tilted back, looking up through the branches of a tall pine. Bernard is gazing at the blue, blue sky, his dark eyes pools that reflect the sunlight peeking through the tree. Just like I used to do, Lottie thinks, always watching the sky and the trees and the squirrels and listening to the wind through the pines, waiting for my uncles and my father and my grandfather to come home from hunting and fishing. The Clearing was where we would gather and wait, listen and watch. It was sort of like the white people's church services, only we had no building or pews. Sometimes one of the adults would talk, but it would be more like a poem or a song when we were all out there, gathered like that.

My little, brown pinecone, she thinks, as she watches Bernard tear himself away from his sky-gazing and turn towards the sound of the bus rumbling up the road. He is easy to see now among all the bright-shirted boys and girls, like a patch of bare ground among all the suburban houses with green lawns in the development across the road. That is where Lottie's people's land ended and the others' world began.

Lottie stands in her doorway a moment longer before closing the rickety door to her little cabin. Amos, her husband, left before it was even light out this morning to meet his brothers and go hunting for deer. Her two older sons work in town. Rosemary, Lottie's only daughter and her eldest, is twenty-four now and married to a K-Mart manager. They live two miles down the road, almost in town and in the heart of the grey, green, and white houses with the big lawns.

Rosemary visits Lottie every week, but never asks out loud the question Lottie sees in her eyes. Once Lottie went so far as to say, "Oh, I'm just like an old coyote, I guess. I'd still rather raid trash heaps than eat dog food!" Rosemary had wrinkled up her nose and cut her visit short. She didn't understand her mother anymore, especially since she had grown up and away and been living in a nice, new, big house near town.

Lottie had meant by that comment that she would rather raid the remnants of the Spirit, hidden now, or almost gone, peeking out from under the debris of the housing developments and planned communities. She had thought of the old three-legged coyote she knew. His leg had been lost to a trap when they still permitted such things in the woods across the road. The developers advertised that they would pay $10 a hide for these wiley critters that ate squirrels and mice and dug up lawns going after gophers. They didn't feel the coyotes were compatible with their customers' rhinestone-collared poodles. The poodles ate only dogfood and went on the lawns, leaving their messes exposed and unburied.

Lottie had tried to feed that three-legged coyote, at first some dog food like her big bluetick hound ate. The coyote wouldn't touch that. (She'd seen him out the window at the crack of dawn. He had sniffed disdainfully at the neat pile she'd left for him behind the house, then lifted his leg on it.) Then she'd tried scraps of tasty (to a coyote) entrails from the animals Amos shot. But the old coyote had scorned Lottie's offerings, even though he was stiff and arthritic and unable to run fast enough to catch much anymore.

Lottie had felt a surge of kinship with him one drizzly morning last spring when she'd surprised him out back. She'd been bringing out a bag of trash to where they burned it in a big barrel. There he was, ferreting out the ripest, rankest tidbits from the overflowing trash heap. Quietly, stealthily, almost reverently, he wrestled them from the pile. The old coyote wouldn't have eaten them had Lottie left them easily accessible. He was stalking what was left of his old way of being. He was hunting the spirit of his survival.

Ah, yes, Lottie had thought, I'm very much like that coyote; she pulled on her old, patched Mexican sweater, on her way out to wander through the forest in search of scraps of kindling and whatever else she could find. Lottie often came home with crushed pieces of plants in her deep pockets: horehound, mullein, fresh pine needles. These would make soothing teas on the cool mornings to come. Rosemary brought her colorful boxes of plant teas (herb teas, Rosemary would correct her) so Lottie wouldn't have to root around "out in those bleak woods," as she put it.

"But I like wandering around out there, seeing what I can find," Lottie would protest. She could see Rosemary shaking her head, thinking her mother was getting to be an old, half-crazy, Indian baglady.

This morning, Lottie walks around, occasionally looking through the sparkling trees, diamonds of sunlight glittering above her head. It is anything but bleak out here this morning. The wind whistles through the high branches, singing the age-old song of mountains and sunlight, mountain lion and bear, eagle and hawk. Life and change, Lottie thinks. The mountains are still here, but worn down with the burden of all those houses on "choice pine lots."

The mountain lion and bear are all but gone, except for a few tucked away in the crevices between Indian lands, national forest, and suburbia. The eagles are long vanished even though they could fly above it all. Lottie feels it must have changed their spirit irretrievably to have to look down and see it all. Even though the mice and rabbits proliferate under the bushes and hedgerows of the manicured lawns, the eagles can't satisfy their voracious appetite for freedom swooping down on even the most open suburban expanse. The strange animals that live encased in solid, spirit-crushing boxes of aluminum siding and brick are there, too close. It is these strange animals' imprisonment that frightens the eagles, Lottie knows, not the animals themselves.

Lottie remembers seeing the eagles swoop across the sky as a child, close to the circle of her people gathered in the old clearing as they swayed and laughed under an afternoon sky. They were like the trees; their song of conversation whooshed through the forest like the trees' song, singing of a life that had by now all but disappeared. Their house had had walls of mountain and a roof of cloud. Sunlight and fresh air had filled the rooms of their life. Rain and snow, cold and wet, washed and cleansed the sins of their survival. It was shared with the others: lion, bear, rattlesnake, and forest mice. They, the Indians, The People, were just one of the many kinds of animals to live there. It was everyone and everything's house.

Lottie muses on what has been given to her and Amos and their children, too, in lieu of that House of Life. The house is not actually gone, she knows, but it is changed enough so that even those who have not lived there with her people feel the vast difference. She knows they see it in her people's faces, in their eyes that reflect the flashing neon bar signs at the edge of town. If you look really close, those eyes also reflect the moist, disappearing earth in their dark, almost black, irises.

Yes, Lottie muses, what is given us? Little pieces of paper with printed numbers, paper that means so much to the others. We can go live in a big, green-and-white house like Rosemary's with that paper. We can trade it for new trucks and shiny, bright clothes from K-Mart, where Rosemary's husband Edward works.

Edward had told Lottie once that these clothes were made out of polyester and needed no ironing. Lottie had never ironed a thing in her life.

"What is polyester?" Lottie had asked.

"Oh, I don't know. A synthetic. It's made out of oil, out of old dinosaur bones," Edward had laughed. "You don't have to hunt and kill the animals like your people have had to, to make clothing."

Oh, Lottie had thought, your clothes are made out of dead, long-dead, rotted animals. No wonder you get no strength from them. She had watched Edward lift a can of beer to his lips, his hand soft and pink. Your food, it is from dead things, too. The meals Rosemary fixed out of boxes and cans when Amos and Lottie came over to eat with them always made Lottie's stomach hurt.

"And all the animals would be gone, hunted and gone, if we all used them to make clothes and eat, like you Indians did!" Rosemary's husband had warmed to the subject as he had finished off his fourth beer that night, the night Lottie and Amos had gone over to visit.

"I have noticed all the animals are almost gone since your people built that new K-Mart down the road last year," Lottie had replied. "There were always enough animals to share their spirit with us, to feed us and clothe us, before . . .before these times," she paused. "And we only had as many of us as there was room in the world for all of us to be!" Amos and she had left then, Rosemary piling boxes of teas into Lottie's arms as she walked them to the door.

"Don't mind Edward, he's a little drunk. He needs to unwind, he's had a tough week at work."

Lottie had nodded and gently touched her daughter's hand in farewell. She had been whisked back by a sudden memory to the sight of her grandfather and father and uncles sitting around the fire after the day was over. They were tired from gathering logs for another dwelling. They were laughing and teasing each other about the day's events. Her grandfather always ended the conversation by mock-complaining: "There aren't enough hours from sunrise to sunset to feel all the sunshine I want to feel on my face," he would boom out, exhilarated. Lottie remembers being a little girl then, drifting off to sleep with the sound of the men's voices in her ears, mixed with the voice of the wind coming off the eaves.

No, Amos and I cannot trade that paper for the return of our home on the earth; Lottie knows somehow that that could never be. She remembers hearing somewhere that trees are cut down, huge forests destroyed, to make the paper that the others so value. With all their paper, they could buy anything they wanted, except, she knows, those vanished lands of giant trees and everything that comes with them. All the animals, all the open sky, the sun and wind and rain that make it home.

Lottie's thoughts scurry like capricious squirrels as she bends over to caress a tiny plant. Amos and I are considered crazy, loco. Even many of our own people feel sorry for us. We live in this shanty of old logs, logs my grandfather and father cut down and drug here so many years ago to be near the edge of the Big Clearing. On stormy nights, the wind whistles right through some of the wall cracks. We need to hear the wind, that's why we stay. It's like an old song that reminds us of yesterday. We take our paper we get each month and use some of it to buy food and clothing, though not the dead spirit kind. But sometimes Amos just goes out in the woods behind the house and throws fistfuls of it into the air, tears running down his cheeks.

He had done that once last winter when I had said I needed some of it to go into town to buy beans and rice and cornmeal. He had run outside that night and I had followed him. He had shouted something into the wind, and the wind had taken all that paper and swirled it up and away into the darkness. He had said, "Now I've given it back to the forest, and the forest will let me find food for us tomorrow." I had been scared and hadn't said anything.

Amos had left early the next morning. He had taken his rifle and two bean sacks, one with the rest of the bread and the last pieces of deer meat in it. I had searched the yard when it got light and found a few pieces of the paper, wet and soggy, coated with icy dew. I had brought them into the house and dried them by the fire and thought how I would walk into town later and get as much beans and rice as I could. But when the paper dried out, I couldn't pick it up and put it in my pocket and go to town, even though I was hungry. I had just thrown the paper in the fire and let it burn. When the ashes were cool that afternoon, and Amos had still not returned, I had gone outside and scattered the ashes on the ground, back in the trees.

Amos had come home two nights later, his face tired but happy. Like me, he had eaten nothing the last day and a half, but he had part of a deer in one sack and one small javelina in the other. I had made a stew with some of the javelina meat and a few potatoes that I had left in a bag in the corner of the room. I had fed Bernard some of those potatoes while Amos was gone. Bernard had never complained or even asked me why he was eating potatoes for breakfast and taking them to school for lunch, too. After school, he had wandered in the forest and returned with piñon nuts to roast, to have with his potatoes.

Lottie hears the bus pulling into the clearing up the road as she climbs the slight rise behind the cabin on her way home. Her frayed bean sack is filled with kindling, and her pockets bulge with plants. She catches the old coyote by surprise again as she emerges from the treeline in back of the house. He is standing there, chewing contentedly on a piece of refuse from the trash heap, the dogfood Lottie had scattered by the trash bin almost untouched. But he has eaten a few bites. Lottie is sure there is less now than what she had left out there this morning.

Ah, yes, I'm like you, old coyote, Lottie sighs. I take what I can from what they've left us, a small, earthy rubble here and there throughout the land. And I nibble at their offerings, too. I went into town yesterday and bought more bread and milk. I just can't take it *all* from them when I still have the freedom to root around to find my own. Amos and I will stop hunting the Spirit when there are no more hunting grounds for the Spirit to flee to. Then you and I, old coyote, will be more than ready to leave. You cannot live in the others' backyards no more than I can live in their houses.

Bernard comes running up to Lottie then, a candy bar in one hand, a giant pine cone clutched in the other. "Mama, will this grow another tree?" he asks. "There are still some pine nuts in it."

"I don't know, Bernard," Lottie answers. "Those pine nuts might be all dried out, but we can try."

"Mama, when there are no more trees, we'll be all gone."

"I know, Bernard."

"My teacher told me that. When there are no more trees, I don't even want to be here! The clearing would be all gone."

Lottie walks into the house, a small, sad smile on her face. I wonder if they will think Bernard is crazy like us, one day, she asks herself. I wonder if Bernard likes candy better than pine nuts. I wonder if all the trees disappear, will the others, the ones who make paper out of trees so they can buy all they want, be gone too?

Amos

Amos, an old man now, squatted in the clearing in the center of the little valley, watching the deer nibble delicately on the bushes not a dozen yards away. Watching, waiting, he could stay still for hours. Praying, he supposed, in a way. Feeling the big sky overhead and the trees gathered around him, he knew this was home. Many a sub-zero night, even now, he'd lie out in his blanket, warm and snug against the earth despite the cold. He had overheard the tourists in the summer, down in town, exclaim over the tales of the Indians camping out in all kinds of weather, even on the bitterest winter nights. They suppose we are used to it, he thought.

He didn't know, but the spirit of the night, whispering through the trees and shining from the stars, made him feel warm and safe. Yet the town, nudging right up against his old cabin, could send chills of hopelessness down his spine on the warmest summer nights. The hum of tires and engine sounds, mixed with the strange laughter that seemed so joyless to him, would rumble through the night air into his house. Then Amos would wake Lottie and they would sneak out through the trees in the blackness of those nights. They would walk far enough from town until nothing of that fearful night could be heard, just their own beating hearts. On many such nights they had listened to the creek running down between the hills and heard the crackling movements of the animals of the night. They had lain naked on pine needles, letting the earth make love to them in piney whispers and soft night breezes. Only then had they turned and, with fear-freed hearts, made love to each other.

Now, as he sat in the sun, the deer gathered in a group around Amos and wandered off, lazily walking on either side of him. They did not see or even smell his rock-silent form that was one with the earth on which he squatted. Amos had become just another of the brown boulders scattered down the side of the mountain and across the valley floor. He felt joy knowing he could become part of the peace of this place.

He was still an excellent hunter. Amos knew, if need be, he could go into the forest and up through the surrounding hills any time he wanted and return with one of the deer. He would stalk them and let himself feel the change he was making in their world. Then one warm deer carcass would be taken down from the hills on his back. Amos would be thankful for this food and look up into the sky, feeling the Spirit nodding its consent.

Some of the other Indians who lived up here took hunters from the cities out to hunt with them. The Indians got money for helping the men find deer, sometimes even chasing the deer within rifle range. But Amos knew that the Spirit was disturbed and angry with such behavior. Those hunters weren't hungry enough to learn the lessons of the deer.

But Amos was out here today to hunt the spirit with his camera. He was fascinated by the images that came out on the shiny 4x4 pieces of paper. He had many albums now, full of fuzzy, out-of-focus shots of trees and mountains, clouds and birds. He even had one with a blurry dark spot in the corner that he told people was the retreating backside of a bear. He laughed when he showed that one.

Amos told his children those pictures were for them and their children, so when he was gone, they could remember what he saw. Rosemary, his eldest, had given him a beautiful volume of color photographs of the forested country in their part of the state one year for his birthday. Amos had looked at this book very carefully as they all watched. He had seemed neither excited nor pleased.

"Thank you, Rosemary," he had said at last that day. "But I cannot see these places; I wasn't there to take these pictures." With that, he had handed the book back to Rosemary and gone to bed.

It lay on the floor by his chair for a long time, unopened, until one of his sons, Bill, came over with his own little son, Wolfie. Wolfie was only two and loved to look at those expensive pictures of white winter mountains, blue sky with green-and-gold horizons. He tore and stained many of the pages of that book, but Amos was glad to let him play with it. When he got older, Amos would show him his pictures of hills and mountains, fuzzy deer and the blurry backside of the bear.

Amos had walked into town with Lottie to buy some groceries one snowy day years ago when he was much younger, and that was when he had bought the camera. They were passing the K-Mart, their heads bent against the grey cold of the building, when Lottie said she needed to go inside and use the bathroom. Amos never liked to go in there; the smells of all the new synthetic clothing made him sad. Ever since Eddie, Rosemary's husband, had explained that the clothing was made from long-dead animals, oil that came from dinosaurs, Amos had felt sad. He knew machines made this clothing, and it felt dead. These clothes had no memory in them, no spirit, like the warm wool sheared off the sheep, or the warm golden light that bounced off the coat of the leaping deer.

While Lottie had been using the bathroom, Amos had wandered around the aisles idly looking at the merchandise. A young salesman had come up behind him, and when Amos had heard him and turned around, the salesman had held up something that went click.

"Would you like to buy a camera today? They're on sale, and I took your picture to show you how good they work!"

As soon as Amos had gotten over being startled, he stared at the slowly forming Polaroid picture of himself. It showed a short, stocky, dark-eyed man with a confused, sad look on his face. He looked troubled.

"This is not me!" Amos had shouted, and the young man had stepped back and started to apologize. "You cannot take a picture of me in here, in this store, with all this death around! I am not here. You could only take a picture of me where I feel free and happy, so the Spirit will come out. This is not me!" Amos grabbed the picture and held it up to the saleman's face. "See! This is a trapped animal who needs to go back to the Spirit to live."

The salesman had tried to step back, to excuse himself from Amos, but Amos stopped him. "But you are right, I *do* want one of these cameras. I will take pictures of where I *am*, so I can remember when I am not there. And my children, who might not be able to remember where they are at all, will be able to see where their father was. Where a human being can be. Thank you. Here. Here is the money!" Amos had pulled the paper out of his pockets, crumpled bills stuffed in with little pieces of wire and bent nails. He had taken the same camera the salesman had set down on the counter and walked over to where Lottie had been standing and watching.

"Come. We will get your flour and other groceries. Then we will go home."

Amos and Lottie had walked the three miles to their cabin slowly up out of town through the six inches of new snow that day, many years ago. Her heavy shawl over her head, Lottie had carried one sack of groceries as Amos had trudged beside her carrying the other. Nestled on top of his sack was the camera. He had spoken to Lottie on and off, trying to explain why he had bought the camera.

"I know one day the town will be everywhere. I will have a hard struggle to see myself with those big buildings and long roads with lines of cars running over me. When I step on the ground, or sit on a boulder, and see sunlight glint off the mountaintop, I see me. But the pavement masks me; I get choked and hidden from myself.

"I know I can get very angry and do something so another man will kill me. Then I will see myself too. But I'm not ready to die. I want to take pictures of what is me. When there are no more pictures, then I will be ready to go."

Lottie had nodded her head and motioned for Amos to stop. She had put down her bundle and pulled Amos under a low-hanging tree, back from the road. "I know, Amos. I love seeing you. And when I can't see you anymore it will be time for you to go on. I am glad you are preparing to journey in peace for as long as you can. We will know when we are done here."

As the snow had gotten thicker, no cars passed them any longer on the road. A foot of snow blanketed the path leading off the road up to their cabin. When they reached it, Amos set the sacks inside the door. Then he had taken his camera and brushed off the coating of snow that had fallen inside the bag. He stepped outside again and stood in the late afternoon light, muffled and silvery with fallen snow. He held the camera up and looked through the lens. Amos saw the faraway stillness that he felt inside himself. He clicked the shutter and watched in awe as the snapshot grew brighter and brighter until it showed a distinct whiteness with fuzzy outlines of snow-laden trees in the distance. My first picture, he thought; this is how I feel. He had stomped his boots and gone back inside then. Lottie had started a fire and was shaking her long, damp hair loose to dry.

Amos remembered what he had said to Lottie back then, on that day many years ago. "Lottie, you know, I've heard town people say everything gets silenced in a heavy snow. It blankets the ground and muffles their words and all their machines. But I can hear the voice of the earth so clear and strong out there now. Even in town the earth speaks when their world gets quiet. Look, I took a picture of it."

Amos's favorite animal had always been the deer. He knew most of the men who lived around this area were more proud to hunt bear or mountain lion or elk. Even the near-sighted, prickly, ugly-beautiful javelina was respected as a fair foe by these men. The deer, though regarded as a source of good food and warm clothing, was not an animal to make one's hair stand on end. Now men marveled at the deer's beauty and grace, then shot him down from a long distance and hacked off the prized rack.

Amos, in his wanderings, had often come across the stiff, still bodies left by the side of some back road, the eyes staring blankly at what they could no longer see. When he encountered such a thing, Amos felt a chill pass over him, even if it was a warm day. He had killed many a deer since he was a young boy, but never had he killed them without need, without feeling.

When he encountered these corpses, he would sit down by the cold body, pull out his pouch of tobacco, and roll a small, crude-looking cigarette. Before leaning back against an embankment or tree to inhale, he would always first take a handful of the tobacco and scatter it around the deer. Amos could feel the spirit of the deer being soothed by his offering. Afterwards, he often sat in front of the deer and looked into the great, gentle eyes that were dead but seemed to watch him. Amos envied the deer then, for it had at last outrun the encroachment of a world all beings like himself and the deer must run from.

On one occasion, he had sat for a long, long time there, next to a slaughtered deer, which he had found lying on a little-used pathway going up the side of Eagle Mountain. As he sat there, the anger, the fear, the frustration had slowly drained out of his tense body. He had felt his despair sinking with the setting sun that day, as the sky had turned streaks of purple and fiery red. Amos had been out hunting, seeking as he did so often of late, not an animal, but the spirit of all the animals, including himself. He had as his weapons, a ravenous heart and his by now well used and battered camera.

He had held the camera in both hands while looking through the scratched lens. He had begun to tremble as a loud, roaring north wind shook the bushes and trees around him. Finally, he had been shaking so badly that he had gotten down on his knees, then on his stomach, hugging the earth that had become his own trembling body.

Amos had still been holding the scratched plastic camera when he knew that the Spirit had found him, had been hunting him all along. It had rolled over him and whistled through his unblinking eyes. He had felt it rushing down his face in a warm, wet torrent. Through the blur of the lens he had seen himself. He wasn't aware when his hand had pressed down the button and had caught the fleeting image. No one had ever found that picture of the staring face of the dead deer until after Amos himself had died.

Amos came wearily into the old cabin. It was now many seasons since that spirit-shaking incident on Eagle Mountain. He sat down heavily in his worn chair by the fire. Lottie walked over and rubbed his stiff shoulders. They were still strong but she could tell Amos was tiring; he was not going out as often anymore. The urgency to climb so frequently up through the pine-clad hills to the top of the mountain had dwindled. That urgency had made Amos almost believe he could outrace the confines below those icy heights where the wind cut through him like a knife.

"That wind almost tears my heart right out of my chest and sets me free," he once told Lottie.

"Yes, I can see that," she smiled, "but that freedom scares me, too!"

Amos had crushed Lottie close to him then after he'd said that, and looked over her head, out through the cabin's window that framed Eagle Mountain. It was disappearing in the fading light. "When I am free, I will have your hand in mine and will take you with me," he whispered.

Now on this night he was very tired. He had taken no pictures today, he told Lottie. Amos had not climbed the mountain at all today, but just gone over the low hills behind their cabin. He had entered the broad tree-trimmed valley beyond, the grasses gold now in the early fall. Amos had walked until he was right in the valley's center and sat there in the golden light of the afternoon. Not one shadow fell upon him the whole day. He had sat stock still and watched the coyotes and deer wander out from the trees. They had seen his still form, like an old stump in the middle of the clearing, and cautiously walked a safe distance around him. He had felt full of peace at last.

This night, as the moon rose, he sat a long time in his chair by the fire. Lottie asked him if he was hungry, but he shook his head. Amos motioned for her to sit by him. Lottie felt the pictures of his day's walk in his mind; she could almost see them flare up like the logs in front of them, lighting the darkened room, warming them both.

Finally, Amos turned to Lottie and asked if she would go down the road and use the neighbor's phone. "I want you to call all our children and have them come here tonight." Lottie didn't ask why, but Amos could see the question in her shoulders as she pulled her sweater around her. "Tonight, you must take my picture," he said.

When Lottie returned, Amos was on the couch, a large, brightly patterned blanket pulled up to his chin.

"Are you so tired, Amos?" she asked. "Bernard and Rosemary will be here very soon. Bill and Buck will be a little longer."

"I can wait," he told Lottie and closed his eyes to rest.

By the time everyone had arrived, the full moon was halfway across the sky. Amos opened his eyes and looked peacefully around the small room. "I am very happy now and I feel very strong. I know now I can run and outdistance all the world. Even our world must be outdistanced in the end. Lottie, I think you should take my picture, now. I am lying here but I am almost to the top of the mountain. Take the picture when I reach the top."

Bernard, the youngest, handed Lottie the old camera. They all watched Amos look around one last time. His gaze fixed on the window nearest him. He could feel more than see the old three-legged coyote out there in the moonlight. "It's a good night to run," he whispered. The words hung softly in the still room. Even the fire seemed to hold its breath. Amos, his face strong and smooth, clutched his chest under the cover. Then he closed his eyes. Lottie quietly took his last picture. She didn't realize until a full minute later that Amos's chest was very still under his bright blanket. His spirit flew into the flames, and they crackled loudly again.

WINDWALKER. AMOS'S SONG

High mountain sky and no white men,
The coyotes howling by their den,
Now I'm old but that was when
I ran with the wind.

Tipi shadows in full moonlight,
Fires dying to embered nights,
My brothers held their women tight,
Young, I rode the wind.

On the wind I heard the trees,
The wind told tales of those who flee,
The wind brought all her strength to me,
Strong, I knew the wind.

In all I am, the wind I feel,
The elk and bear gave gifts to heal,
I have had young but now I hear
This message on the wind.

The wind blows through my oldening hide,
The scream of lion on wind blows by,
Though I've hunted well, I'll slow and die,
I'll, too, blow on the wind.

High mountain sky I still can see,
And the woman who came along with me,
And all my animal-brothers that be,
But a change is on the wind.

The wind completes the circle of time,
Asks back from me the strength that's mine,
Caresses me to sleep beneath the pines,
I leave upon the wind.

A great strong medicine is the wind,
Friend and foe alike, she takes back again,
We dance together as her voice sings,
All borne upon the wind.

Bernard

I almost stumble in my half-crouch gait, as I weave my way down the side of Eagle Mountain. I am so intent on watching the doe with her two-month-old fawn, paralleling their descent, that I scarcely notice the terrain in front of me with all its loose rocks. I have on the moccasins I made, rugged soft booties put together like my grandmother showed me when I was no more than seven or eight. They aren't sewn with the same skill, but I tanned this particular hide myself, from a buck I shot two falls ago. They are very supple; I can feel the earth beneath my feet. This helps me sense the connection between my people and myself and my present life, in town as I am many days, wearing hard cowboy boots that make my feet numb.

That's why I almost stumble. Though my people might boast of being closer to this earth, I am distanced by the times and the in-between world I live in. That's why my feet don't know the earth as well, don't have the awareness to sidestep the loose rocks and feel secure on the slick pine needles. I have practiced walking silently, invisibly, up and down this mountain, but I know I don't blend in like my grandfather, or even my father, did. I even smell different. Last night in Smokey's Bar clings to me in the crevices where neither the sun and the wind, nor even the old dances and stories, can reach. The mountain tolerates my attempts to fit in, perhaps taking pity on this half-spirited, if full-breed, son.

The doe bolts, the fawn at her side shielded from harm. Even though I catch myself in time—I hear no telltale skittering of pebbles—the doe has felt me. My spirit has faltered, and she knows I am not one with the mountain.

I am not hunting; at least, I have no gun or knife. But I am hunting in a way, I realize. I am stalking the elusive spirit of this spot: the pines, the sky, the wind *and* the deer. The spirit can flee even more quickly than a startled animal. I feel tears running down my face, icy in the brisk fall wind.

I have seen white hunters cuss and moan when they miss their last chance to bag a splendid buck. I feel much worse than that. The deer are all around, and I know how to read their signs and follow their prints. The soft hides and proud racks are always within reach for me. In that way I am a good hunter.

But I feel like an unfaithful lover who realizes too late I will never, ever, be trusted again with that first innocent trust by the beloved. I've done wrong, if only in my own innocently ignorant way—a child lured by older, cleverer children, whose more sophisticated pleasures blot out the original joy of just being.

I've betrayed something in myself, and by that I've betrayed her, the damp living earth under my clumsily moccasined feet. Even if she can forget, I can't. I know I'll never be the lover my grandfather and his generation were, and I cry for this. The earth unjudgmentally soaks up my tears. I see the treetops, sky, and mountain itself when I look up and outward; but they are blurred, out of focus in my stumbling heart. I can smell the beery stink in my hair from last night. I run all the way down to the creek flowing in and out of Eagle Mountain's toes and throw myself in.

"Bernard, you look cold!" Mama's voice greets me as I push open the old cabin's door. She has lived here always; as a child this was her parents' home. She hands me a warm wool poncho that is her outer skin, no matter the weather. "Did you fall in?" Almost immediately she regrets her words. Bernard, her youngest son, her barfly, half-cowboy, half-Indian son, would never fall in no matter how clumsy his spirit seems. She knows this and silently hands me a cup of steaming tea, pine-needle tea from needles gathered this morning.

"Thanks, old Indian woman," I say with deep affection. I grin and wink at her. She is grateful to be an *old* Indian woman. This means she is closer to what was, when our world was still in focus, than I will ever be, no matter how good I make moccasins or how silently I try to walk.

I stay the night, which is probably more than my two older

brothers or sister will ever do. They visit for the cursory hour or two on special occasions, but that's all they can bear. They have all but forgotten the smells and sounds; that must be how they like it. To remember any clearer what seems to be just a brief dream in the white man's busy day, sets one apart and adrift. No point in getting old *and* crazy before your time.

But I can't help immersing myself in it when I come to visit. I always say, "No, I can't stay, old mama, I have somewhere else to go." But I do often stay. The hours drift by; the pink-and-gold evening sky behind Eagle Mountain dulling my pain more than the beer in Smokey's Bar can ever do. Its mountain-ness soothes me. It sings old songs to me in the night through the cracks in the cabin's walls. I rock back and forth in front of the fire with my dead father's poncho over my shoulders. I fly through the flames with the old man.

I remember being as close as I've ever been to where we come from when the two of us walked through Eagle Gap on the far side of the mountain. It was during the icy winter before he left. I felt the swoosh of the wind at our backs as we trudged through the pass in the moonlight. The ground was icy-slick under the pine needles, but I was warm with him on those nights. I could feel the thudding heart of the mountain inside his chest when we unrolled our blankets to bed down. We lay close together on the pallet of needles we made against a snowy hillside. I looked up at the stars as I scrunched down into the earth, against my father, and it was all in focus. The world felt whole and, when the sun rose the next morning, we were part of it.

Nowadays, with my father gone, I can't hear the close thud-thud of the mountain's heart; it doesn't matter how carefully I listen, even when I get out of town and away from Smokey's Bar. It's fuzzy when I try to see it clearly, like a permanent hangover, even if I haven't been in town for days.

I wake up early that next morning after my dreams in front of the fire at my old mother's house. I feel light-headed and disoriented, like I've drunk too much beer and tequila the previous day. But I know it's only the wild nightmare I've ridden down the old path leading from my world into this sunny, hot, tortilla-scented daybreak.

My mother is across the room, over the stove cooking our

breakfast. We sit down together with tea, tortillas, honey, and eggs from her chickens. For a moment I feel whole.

"I must go soon, old Mama, really. They expect me back at Cy's place today to help tear down the old fence in the pasture."

"Yes," she says. She looks happy seeing me sitting here, for one moment looking clear and content. "I wish the old fence inside you could come down that easy." She pats my hand and adds, "But I'm glad you hop over it from time to time, eh, little pinecone?" That's my old childhood name she's called me. "Perhaps you fell in the stream yesterday, jumping over that fence?" She chuckles to herself, and her eyes look bright, dark and shining like the muddy creekbank. I think she tags along with me during those times, making sure I don't catch myself on the wire's barbs.

I rise slowly and stretch in the patch of sunlight falling across the kitchen area where we've been sitting. The sunlight looks clearer here, through the dusty cabin window, than in any of the houses I've stayed in in town.

"Goodbye, Mama." I hug her for a long time, memorizing the feel of her poncho-skin and the sight of the log walls. I will need to see this when I'm at Smokey's, falling through the fuzzy, smoke-filled air inside the bar.

I bounce over the rutted road that winds its way down into Cy Lamont's ranch. He is an old friend: we stood together many a chilly morning waiting for the school bus. It's really his father's ranch, but his father is dying. "Goin' off to that other land," as Cy would sometimes say when we were out walking around his place, fixing fences, counting cattle, or just watching the sky, wondering if it would rain.

"What's that other land like, Cy?" I asked him once. We were squatted down looking at javelina prints in the mud by the creek.

"Oh, I don't know, Bern. If it isn't much like here though," he paused and trailed his sunburned hand in the cool water, "I ain't much interested in goin'."

So I could see we had something in common. Cy loved the trees and mountains too, even if he didn't walk very quietly through the woods when we hiked around out there together. He came from a long line of people who'd noisily and aggressively knocked down the trees and scared or hunted off all the animals.

They even pushed back the mountains, it seemed, with their big square houses that loomed on the skyline across the surrounding hills. But he loved the mountains more than the houses on them. As a kid he would beg me to show him my people's paths. We'd take off after school and on weekends and I'd take him back in the forest, behind where I lived.

"Oh, is this one of your people's trails?" he'd want to know, pointing to a deer trail, sometimes even an old cow path, that criss-crossed through the underbrush.

"Sure, sure," I'd laugh, glad just to be out there, sniffing around like a coyote pup in the springtime. Once we'd even startled a shaggy little black bear, when there was still a few left around there.

"Hey, Bern, let's get outta here!" he'd yelled. The bear took off in one direction, and we ran in another. We ran and ran through the hills, leaping across arroyos, finally climbing onto a ledge partway up Eagle Mountain. Panting, we fell on our backs and started up into the blue October sky.

"You know, I think we're lost, Bern," Cy had at last said, when he'd gotten his breath back and was sitting up looking around.

"Nah, that was one of my people's paths we were following," I couldn't help answering, trying not to laugh.

"Oh." Cy gave me a funny sidewise glance but never asked about deer trails or cow paths again. I think he got the idea that my people's paths, like a young boy's, were wherever you felt moved to run, leap, or climb.

He loved to come and visit in my parents' dwelling when we were in school. He told me once that time seemed to go slower there as he watched my mother flatten out her tortillas and mash beans for dinner. "Your days seem longer," he'd sigh, stretching out on our braided rug floor. "Your fire has magic in it. You have cracks in your walls, and it isn't even cold in here."

"Don't you have a warm fire?" I'd asked him once.

"Yeah, but our house is too big to feel close to it."

I wondered about that one time when we were older. We were teenagers, drinking beer around a fire. It was the end of a long day's trek through the hills. We were camping out, our first overnight hunting trip alone.

"It's big out here, Cy, but I feel close to this fire."

"It's big out here, all right," he nodded, "but I feel like I fit in here. Like I'm close to everything."

"Yeah, I know what you mean." I fell asleep, looking at the path of my people, way up above me, in the stars.

Tearing the fence down is a hard job. I sweat as Cy and I jerk on those rotted posts, seemingly grown right down into the earth, like ancient tree roots. We cuss and yell, stubbing toes and puncturing fingers. We kick violently at those crazily leaning posts, which won't budge without at least a half-hour of bad language. We rip jagged tears in our gloves pulling that old barbed wire off and tossing it in the back of my truck. We finally quit after five hours of this carrying on. It is almost dark, getting damp and cold as the light fades.

"Let's go into town and grab a few," Cy mutters, throwing the last post in the truck with a vengeance. "We deserve it."

"Sure." I am glad to call it a day, to wipe off my last bloody tear from the damned wire and hop in the truck.

We lurch back up the hill and across the lumpy pasture in the dark. I turn the truck onto the relatively smooth road that leads through the ranch gate and down into town, fifteen miles away. We are at Smokey's by seven-thirty, and I anticipate a long, beery night. Grabbing a corner table, we sit there for a few minutes, deciding what to eat with our beer.

We stay there almost until closing at eleven. I have eaten my burritos hours ago but I'm still working on a beer. I have lost count, but I don't care as long as things stay sufficiently fuzzy. Cy slouches across from me with an Indian girl we both went to school with. She is making eyes at him.

"Deena, you're a pretty girl," I hear myself saying, "so what do you want with a white man like him?" I laugh as I say it. We know we are all white at heart, even though we sit in a place like this and carry on like drunk Indians.

"You sure can drink enough beer for an Indian," Cy snorts back at me. He has had even more than me; I can tell by how lopsided he looks.

"Well, you sure can tear down fences for a white man!" I counter, laughing, slapping him on the back. Then I feel my eyes growing moist. "Hey, I gotta go, no more beer."

I stumble out into the night. The stars look fuzzy, then clear, as I blink my eyes. Drops of water fall into the gravel where I stand; it soaks up the tears as unjudgmentally as the ground on the mountain did. I didn't use any faded visions of my people to avoid falling through the smokey air in the bar tonight. I didn't need any more beer, either, to fog up the night—that was mine, or anyone's, to see as *I* liked.

ROSEMARY

Rosemary smoothed back her long dark hair. She stood in front of the bedroom mirror. Her vanity table held the various turquoise and tortoiseshell combs she used to hold back her thick, heavy hair. Rosemary ran her coppery hand along the vanity's edge, marveling at its size. As a child, she, her parents, and her brothers had eaten at a table no larger than this. She felt both apprehension and longing, remembering those days that she had worked so hard to put behind her. In reality, she was only thirty-one, but she wanted those aching memories to be a full life's distance from her trembling Indian heart.

She had worked diligently to tuck that world neatly and safely behind her carefully coiffed present life. Working as a buyer for the store her husband managed, she did her job with a vengeance. The strands of Rosemary's past were as precisely tucked away as was her hair every morning in preparation for her workday. And just like her hair, she went to great lengths to disguise its flowing Indian-ness. But never would she cut it off. Behind the rush of buying, ordering, and stocking the store where she worked, Rosemary knew it was the past that gave her the strength to be what she was in her present life.

She glanced one last time in the mirror, noticing with approval how her dark hair complimented her pale delicate blouse. As she strode confidently out of the room, she paused by the hall phone to write herself a note. She needed to call Lottie, her mother, tonight and invite her for dinner tomorrow. She and Edward could pick Lottie up after work; perhaps they would be able to convince her to spend the night. If not, they'd drive Lottie back to her small weathered cabin on the edge of the reservation.

Amos, her father, was gone now; he had died a few years ago of a heart attack. At least, that's what the doctor in town had said.

"No, his heart just decided to stop fighting the attack of your world on it!" Lottie had vehemently replied when the doctor told her this.

Rosemary, standing beside her mother at the time, smiled a bitter smile through her tears. She heard herself say, "He didn't know how to fight those battles, but look, Mama, he held his own until the end."

It was true. Lying on the bed with all his family around him, the blanket pulled up to his chin, Amos had looked as smooth and strong as the old kettle of Lottie's on the woodstove. His own heart hadn't attacked him; it had just stopped when it had realized the world of the development across the road was here to stay, that there was no battling the traffic, noise, and confusion of the new day which Amos had lived to see.

"He will come back if he needs to. . . " Lottie's voice had trailed off. She had stood there, staring forlornly through the window at the old three-legged coyote who was nosing through the trash behind the house. Then suddenly, the coyote had sat and let out a low, mournful howl, something he never did. The whole family had turned and nodded their assent.

"Yes, maybe he has found a more convenient way to be here now," Bernard, the youngest, had ventured.

After that day of Amos's death, Lottie left a bowl of whatever she'd made for dinner out for the old coyote. He would come near the house to eat it—something else he had never done before.

Parking behind the store, Rosemary slipped out of her car. She glanced at her large feet, stylishly clad in some low-heeled shoes. Some things just couldn't be disguised; Rosemary's feet were big and broad, made to cover many miles of roving over the forested hills. She hadn't done much of that since she was a child, none since that day as a teenager when she had overheard one teacher exclaim, "But she's an Indian."

Rosemary had been behind the school, waiting in line with eleven other girls to try out for cheerleading. The teacher who had uttered that remark had been surprised to see Rosemary there; he'd been standing with the other teachers there to judge the competition. As he turned to look over at the students there to compete, he had taken in Rosemary's long dark braids and slightly out-of-sync clothes. The words had pierced Rosemary like a carefully aimed arrow.

Rosemary had looked down at her wool skirt with the bright pattern that seemed so natural at home and had realized her mistake, the mistake of being so obviously Indian in a white world.

"Rosemary, where are you going?" her friend Donna had shouted as Rosemary ran, big, awkward, and humiliated, off the field. She had disappeared into the shadow of the school building. She couldn't answer her friend; her humiliation was too great.

Over the weeks after that incident, her humiliation had hardened into determination. It was beyond Rosemary to mold her solid, statuesque frame into a nimble, light-hearted cheerleader. But she could disguise, if not change, some of the differences. She took the meager savings from her summer job helping her brothers and father cut firewood and bought the kind of clothes that softened her stark edges.

Rosemary had begun to look more like the young girls who clerked in the local stores during the holiday season. And in fact, as winter approached, that's what she had found herself doing. She had listened carefully to the conversations of her customers and learned how to talk like them. Rosemary had realized then that her heart, which had savagely, if innocently, raced in wild response to the sky and the wind when she was outdoors roaming the hills with her brothers, was now successfully subdued, its beating muffled under layers of new clothes and new perceptions.

Lottie had been very upset when Rosemary took all that money, saved for the horse she had wanted, and spent it on clothes that neither looked warm nor Indian.

"Mama, that's the point! I'll never get anywhere looking like that. I can get a horse and ride and ride all over these hills and never get anywhere! I need to be more like them."

After hearing Rosemary out, Lottie had walked impatiently outside. She had circled the area behind the house, looking for kindling for the night's fire. She had stopped suddenly to glance skyward, then across the road at the bulldozed development roads. At last she had come back inside, put her hands on Rosemary's shoulders, and squeezed gently. "I remember yesterday, and it's a part of me. I was born then. You were born when this day had already dawned. You must do what you have to, to live in today. I don't want you to hate today. All life has a purpose. Find what this day's purpose is."

Rosemary and Lottie had never talked about this again. Lottie was both sad at the changes in Rosemary and relieved that she was learning to survive in a world she and Amos didn't know or understand.

Rosemary was both annoyed and impatient with her parents and their old ways. She felt anger at their refusal to move into a newer house, like those of her friends, with electricity and plumbing. But she also knew she would be grief-stricken with loss if Lottie and Amos left this place. This knowledge came to Rosemary in the wee hours of the night, when she heard the pine boughs scrape the roof and smelled the wind through the cracks around the window by her bed. Maybe she couldn't stay here, but she needed her parents to remain.

Rosemary had left high school in her last year. She had seen the road to her future in Edward, the man she worked for, and married him. He teased her about being a stone-faced Indian at times, but he admired her determination. She had been promoted to buyer after four years at his store; not because she was his wife, but because she was a strong partner. Rosemary knew that he loved the wind that still blew across her soul, muffled though it was.

She had seen the same thing as a child, in the white men who would drive around selling the real estate across the road. They extolled the virtues of the new community they were planning and exclaimed when they saw a deer or a coyote. They bemoaned the fact that the wild animals were disappearing with no apparent awareness of their role in that process. Edward was like those men. He loved to see her dressed up, and he loved to see her dressed down, her heart naked as a winter sunset. Rosemary would feel pity that he didn't understand both; and anger that he didn't feel the conflict that came with understanding both.

Rosemary called Lottie that night at the neighbor's;. the neighbor hurried the seventy-five yards down the old dusty path between the houses to get Lottie. Rosemary heard the slam of the kitchen door, and Lottie, breathless, picked up the phone.

"Hello, Mama? We want to come get you tomorrow night for dinner. Is that okay? Will you spend the night? It's been two weeks since we've seen you. No, you won't? Is that old coyote still hanging around? Oh, Mama, he doesn't care whether you're home or not! Okay, Mama. See you then. Goodbye."

Rosemary put down the phone, aware of an old familiar annoyance and nostalgia in her mind. She went upstairs, let down her hair, and shrugged out of her pale silky blouse. She was pulling on a worn flannel shirt when Edward came in the room.

"Rose, you look great, but you can't work like that. No Indian buyers." He ran an appreciative hand over her broad shoulders and down her straight back.

"Don't you mean, no Indian givers?" Rosemary shot back, half-playful, half-sullen.

Edward bent over Rosemary and said quietly, "I've never given you anything I took back. The next day, week, year, never." He was stung, more than a little, by her tone and moved partway across the large bedroom.

"I know. It's just that I talked to Mama, and I always feel guilty when I hang up. She's coming for dinner tomorrow but we have to bring her home. The coyote, you know." Rosemary felt the wind in her heart picking up.

Edward came back over and brushed a loose strand of shiny hair off Rosemary's face. He stood there staring at her for a moment, then spoke again.

"Your mama has what she wants, and you took what you wanted, Rosemary. Don't forget that. You never had yesterday's choices and neither did I. And don't forget when you fix dinner tomorrow to make extra for your mama. She'll need to take some home with her for the coyote."

August

August William One Tree looked out over the sea of young Indian faces. A teacher of English as a second language, he felt the boredom, like a grey smoke, hanging in the room's stale air. He slipped his hand into his pocket and took out the bone-smooth object he had brought along today. August was going to explain its history, then ask them to write a poem about it.

Before he could begin, the pipe slipped from his fingers, hit the hard concrete floor, and slid under a front-row desk. A small chip broke off the bowl. As August bent down to retrieve the pipe, he heard the muffled titters coming from the class. Down on all fours, he suddenly realized how silly he looked; August felt himself color with humiliation and rage.

He fought an urge to jump up and shake these sullen high-school students by their necks. "Wake up!" he wanted to shout. "The earth is still beneath your feet! Feel it!" Instead, he walked loudly over to the window, his feet thundering like a white man's. I have no respect for myself. The thought caught him like a hidden snare.

August grabbed the window and shoved hard upward. Too late, he realized the jolt would break the glass. The dull faces snapped around, color and feeling rushing into them before the tinkle of falling glass had stopped.

"It was suffocating in here," August Bill boomed out. "We need to breathe fresh air! I want you all to write what this broken window made you think about." Then he left the room.

His family called him Bill, his Indian family: his mother, two brothers and Rosemary. He had been nine when he had asked them to call him that, and not August, as his mother had named him. His twin brother was Buck. She had named them August and Buck because she had dreamed of them coming to her in August, as they had. She had also dreamed of them being guided by a large, brown-gold deer.

Amos, their father, had come home the night they were born, after three days' hunting on Eagle Mountain. He had told Lottie of the great deer he had seen, leading a group of smaller deer. He had brought home the spirit of that deer, he told her, in a huge antler he had found when that deer and his herd passed. Two hours later, August and Buck were born.

Amos had made two simple yet beautiful pipes out of that antler and given each of the boys one when they turned sixteen. Buck's was quickly stained by the tobacco and marijuana he smoked in it with his friends. August had never used his; it now sat on the mantle over the fireplace in his big house in town.

Bill One Tree walked quietly down the hall outside his classroom, where he had just broken a window. He left his students, unattended, fifteen minutes before the bell rang, signaling the end of class. He slipped out a side door, sprinted across the green, manicured lawn to the parking lot, and got into his car. This could be my job, he thought. But a louder voice answered, This could be your life. He felt a courage and a respect for himself he hadn't felt in years, maybe never. The thought startled him. More than anything he wanted to go out into the woods beyond town and smell the pine-scented air. He turned left on the road out of town and up into the surrounding hills.

Bill didn't know when he first became aware that he had entered the reservation, had passed the turnoff to Lottie's old, rundown cabin, and was almost to the base of Eagle Mountain. He stopped the car at the dirt pullout by the little creek and began to hike upstream, his running shoes soft on the earth and his sport coat flapping gently against his side. A mile or so upstream, he found the spot where a deep pool formed between two granite boulders. He quickly took off all of his clothes, folded them, and layed them neatly on top of his shoes. Then he took a deep breath and plunged into the icy water.

He lay there for a long time, until he could see his father, now six years gone, standing by the stream's edge in the fading August twilight, saying: "Here, Buck and August. You have heard the story of the great deer and your birth sixteen summers ago. You know that deer gave me a gift, the beautiful antler I found. I made these for you from that gift. It is my gift to you now that you are grown. It will help you feel what I felt on that day many years ago, if you let it." Amos had then handed each of the boys a smooth white pipe. Buck had grinned and hugged his father, but Bill had looked away, embarrassed.

Now Bill felt that old embarrassment again and the humiliation of it. He felt all the years of confusion and doubt, those years of taking the schoolbus down the old dirt road, six miles into town, to the white people's school. There, he realized with regret, he had learned how to talk like them, walk like them, eat like them, and finally, when imprinted with the fear of not fitting in, think like them.

Bill felt himself shudder with the chill of knowing he might be a half-baked Indian, but he was an even worse white man. He could give his students no feeling for those ways, which made him stiff and numb, a boring teacher. "Shit!" he screamed out to the still, dark pines on the surrounding hillsides. As he dove under the cold water, he felt his hot tears merge with the icy current. August came up sputtering, laughing, and crying, and feeling warm all over.

It was dusk when he pulled up in front of his white brick house. His hair was plastered back from the water and from the wind beating on him through the open window on the drive back into town. Laramie, his tall, slender wife, waited in the door with three-year-old April. Wolf, the impulsive, defiant eight-year-old who reminded Bill so much of his twin brother was at the car door before he could open it.

"Where you been, Dad? Huh? I wanted you to take me out to Granma Lottie's today after school. Where were you?!"

"Wolf, quiet down! Let me talk to your dad." Laramie was by the car now, her eyes asking the questions she hadn't voiced yet.

"August, the school called me about one and said they couldn't find you. Your English students said you broke a window and left. The school sounded upset and worried but . . ." Laramie paused, her eyes searching out the change in him, "you know I wasn't. I could feel you needed to go someplace you've missed for a long time, but I couldn't tell the school that. You'll have to talk to them."

Laramie was unusual, Bill knew that. She had insisted on calling him August after she had met him and heard the story of his birth from Amos. She was one-quarter Indian, from a grandfather up in Canada, although you couldn't really tell that by looking at her. She had light brown, wavy hair and grey-flecked hazel eyes. But she was different, and "never had made it in the white world," as Laramie had put it when he'd started talking with her on their first encounter.

She had been hitchhiking up through the state that summer nine years ago. You could make it white, Bill wanted to tell her, when she'd said that. Then he'd looked closer. No, no, she couldn't have, and he shook his head. Despite himself he had looked at her from his center, where his spirit stood still. Her hazel eyes locked with his then on that road going north, upstate, and he'd felt relief. In his college days, trying to find a foothold in a shifting world, he knew something Indian had found him, despite his dodging it.

Laramie opened the car door and touched his wind-burned face. He couldn't look directly at her.

"You know, I may not have a job anymore. I went out to the pool, the one where my father gave me the pipe."

"I know. I feel like I've been waiting for nine years for this. I saw that you took your pipe with you today. I knew then something would happen."

"You're more Indian than I am." August finally lifted his head and looked at Laramie. "You knew all along I would come to this."

"I didn't know, August, but I was hoping. This is where I can be closest to you."

August ran a dusty hand through his hair, then grabbed Laramie around the waist. "I'd better go call the school," he said at last.

He told the school he needed a week off. He'd be back, but maybe not to stay, he added. Since he'd been there five years now, the principal said okay but there was a tightness in his voice.

"I just need to sort things out, Joe."

"Yeah, well I've got two other Indian guys who've asked about a job here recently. See, I like you, Bill, but I've got a school to run."

"I've got my life to run and if I can't get it together . . . " Bill was cut off abruptly by his boss.

"You've had it together enough to teach in this damn school for five years. Look, you've got a week off, now. You need to get your perspective tightened up, so do it. See you then!"

"Yeah, tightened up. See ya." Bill banged the phone down. He turned around and caught Laramie looking at him. She looked happier than he could remember seeing her in a long time.

"Lottie wants us to come out for the weekend at least, August. She said Wolf and April could stay with her if we wanted to camp out some. Let's. It's been so long!"

"That sounds good." August felt familiar warmth rising in him.

They threw bags of food and clothing in the car and left the big house. Wolf hung out the back window, grinning from ear to ear, while April sat still on the back seat and clapped her hands every time she saw a squirrel.

Lottie was out front, her arms full of kindling, when August stopped the car by the little cabin. He'd forgotten how old and tiny it was. After college, once he'd left for good, he'd never spent a night here again. The old plank, set across two stumps and passing for a bench, used to hold ten people when he was little. It might hold four, August now realized. He took the kindling from Lottie and pushed open the rickety front door.

The sights and smells overwhelmed him as he set the wood in front of the chipped black stove. The stove had two burners, and though compact, still stuck out in the small front room. Lottie had her big kettle on top, full of beans with deer knuckles.

"Two days," she nodded to Laramie. "They'll be just right tonight."

August sat down in Amos's worn chair, still in its place to the left of the stove. Through the dusty window the ancient mountain glinted gold in the setting sun. August could feel his face flush, hot with the late afternoon sunlight on his cheeks. Lottie was busy by the counter flattening out tortillas; her dark hands were a startling contrast to the yellow cornmeal. Laramie dropped their sleeping bags in a messy pile in the middle of the room. Then she threw herself down on top of them.

"I love it out here, August. For a long time, I've wanted to tell you I'd like to stay out here sometimes with Lottie," Laramie said, looking up at him.

August smiled back at Laramie, then squinting, gazed off into the distance. "We will stay out here with Lottie, with the mountain, whenever we feel like it now."

Lottie was pounding with flour-dusty hands on the countertop a beat that felt familiar and warm. She hummed to herself and gave Wolf and April little pieces of tortilla dough to play with.

August felt the fingers of sunlight slip down his face, still as a twilight caress. He watched the sun disappear behind the mountain. Out of the shadows hopped the three-legged coyote. August was surprised, yet somehow almost expected him.

"Look, Lottie, there's the coyote! You said you hadn't seen him since early summer."

Laramie and the children, like three silent forest animals themselves, slipped over to the window and watched, entranced. The coyote hopped lightly over the pine needles covering the ground until he stood almost right under the window. Then he pulled back his grey lips, showing all his worn down teeth, and grinned. Wolf and April let out shrieks of laughter, and the coyote howled. Then he was gone. Lottie's black eyes sparkled from across the room. "I thought he'd be by here tonight," was all she said, wiping a flour-speckled hand across her damp cheek.

August spent the best week of his life there at Lottie's, up on Eagle Mountain with Laramie. He explored the old mountain—the trails he hadn't been on, since he was young, with Amos and his brothers. He discovered feelings he hadn't felt since he was Wolf's age and had run, leaping and dancing, through the fall woods. He remembered turning summersaults in the golden fall grasses, and then falling down, enchanted, in that hidden valley behind the low hills, in front of the mountain. Now he did it all over again, Wolf and Laramie running alongside him, April on his shoulders. It was magic, even more so than it had been back then, because Laramie and Wolf and April were there with him, and it was now.

Laramie and August were two thirds of the way around the mountain, almost to the pass where they planned to spend the night; Wolf and April were with Lottie. August took their bags off his back, put them down, and patted the ground next to him. Laramie took her day-pack off and flopped down in a patch of sunshine.

"It's different now, Laramie. Oh, I don't mean just because I'm older and have you and Wolf and April. I had my family then, too. Amos was something else—like this old mountain, he'll always be around. I got to see him then, and I feel him now. But back then it was bittersweet, like the sun going down. I was afraid then of all the endings. Right before Amos died and said everything must be outdistanced in the end, even our world, I saw death and Amos's way of looking at things, as a black hole. I hated it and I feared it. Now I see it as a door. Now I feel the sun coming up. Laramie, do you know what I mean?" August stopped, out of breath, out of words.

Laramie was lying in the sunlight, stretching out on the warm earth and pine needles. Her eyes were squeezed tightly shut, but the tears trickled down from the corners. August moved to brush them off with his hand.

"No. They're mine." She opened her eyes and looked at him with a sly smile. "I've held them inside for a long, long time. Way before I met you. Most people want to outwit death and change. I always knew to learn about life you'd have to learn about death!" Laramie laughed and jumped up. "Come on! I want to see Eagle Pass as the sun's going down."

August ended the best week of his life on Eagle Pass, watching the sun go down, feeling the old mountain, the old messages that Amos had so often brought him up here to feel. Laramie seemed to understand and hear, too.

They walked back around the mountain the next day, hiking downward through the trees, back to Lottie's cabin to get Wolf and April. They had to go back into town, back to the white house to live the changes August finally had the courage to feel. On the way down it started to rain—first little, cold drops, then engulfing sheets of water. Lightning sliced the earth as they ran for cover.

Lower down, under the thick bushes, they found a hollowed-out spot in the hillside. August and Laramie crawled in, unrolled the still-dry-inside sleeping bags, and pulled off their wet clothes. They lay there, talking and touching for a long time. Their love-making was just part of the earth's conversation of rain, wind, and fire.

It was late in the night when they finally crawled down from the mountain and reached the warm womb of Lottie's cabin, which was dark and quiet, Lottie and the children long asleep. They crawled together beneath the dry covers on the patched couch where Amos had last lain and listened to the drip off the eaves.

Next day, August, Laramie, Wolf, and April piled into their small car. Maneuvering over the rutted road back into town, August noted that it looked different than it had just a week before. The two realities overlapped and, unlike the death of one, as he had feared, they gave life to each other.

He saw a part of himself sitting by the edge of the road as he pulled away from Lottie's cabin. It was in the trees waving grey limbs overhead, toes curled into the embankment; it was in the grasses choking the edge of the gravel drive. He felt broken and at peace at the same time. The urge to outrun the slowness of eternity returned, as he felt the town closing in around him.

"Laramie, why does time choke the peace out of me here?" August turned to look at her, as they waited at a stoplight.

"Time is choked full of things in this way of living. And we're part of what time is. Just a way to measure life."

"I don't know if I can teach anymore. Why should I be part of this?"

"You already are, August," Laramie cut him off. "There's no undoing what we've already experienced. But I'm ready to feel parts of me I've ignored for a while."

The house felt alien to both of them as they opened the front door. It has been inhabited by ghosts for a long time, August thought to himself. I need to find a real me to live in it. He wasn't used to the uncertain feelings he was having. He wasn't used to feeling, he realized with a jolt. I was so young when I thought I had to be something other than what I was. This thought was new to him, and he suddenly felt very young again, very unused to who he was. Who am I? he wondered, walking through the silent, though not unfriendly, rooms.

Just then the phone rang, and August picked it up to hear his brother's voice, breathing hard on the other end. It had been a year since they'd spoken to each other.

"Buck, where are you? What's up?"

"I need a place to stay for tonight. I know you don't like me around, I blow your image. But I've had some back luck. Made some wrong moves."

"Come on over. I've blown my own image. I did it all by

myself. It's probably the best thing I've ever done."

"Yeah? See ya in a while."

The phone went dead and August felt the room fill up with a liveness, the reality of himself. He didn't know what it was, but it felt good. Buck had always embarrassed and scared him before; Buck was the dark side of life to him, the part that would destroy his chance to be, in a white world. For the first time August knew that he himself was his only chance, and if he couldn't fit in any description, white or Indian, he would make his own.

A half hour later, Buck burst through the door. He was dirty and dusty and a gash, crusted over with dirt and dried blood, sliced across his forehead.

"Bill, I spilled my bike."

"I took a fall myself recently, Buck. It nearly made me crazy, but I'm healing."

The two brothers stopped then, looking strangely at each other. Bill walked over closer to Buck, and they abruptly hugged, slapping each other on the back. Buck stood silent for a moment in his brother's embrace. Then he moved over to the mantle and picked up the chipped pipe.

"I'm starting to listen, Buck. The pipe spoke to me." August walked over quietly and stood behind his brother.

Buck nodded and felt safe with his brother, something he'd never felt before. He began to tell August what had happened to him in the last year.

Buck

You can get comfortable wherever you are if you stay there long enough.

"Shit!" Buck rolled over in the ditch and let his face fall back down into the brittle weeds. A tear down the left side of his jeans exposed his muscular leg from thigh to knee; his leather jacket was shredded over the left shoulder. He brushed his right hand over the tensed muscles and knew the flesh was all right.

He groaned again, thinking of what he could've looked like. Hamburger. Like those dead squashed dogs he passed on the highway sometimes, late at night, their glassy eyes reflecting the bike's headlight. Hamburger with eyes, he thought. Buck ran his unscathed hands across his own face and eyes then, rubbing the dust and gravel out of them. He felt the jagged gash across his forehead, crusted now with dirt and dried blood. "Ugh!" He felt the sound escape him like a rapidly deflated balloon.

The earth under him felt suddenly comfortable and soft, not like the can-and-bottle-littered ditch that it was, but like a warm bed. He pulled his jacket collar up around his long, matted hair, curled into himself, and fell asleep. It was near eleven at night and on this deserted road, no one would disturb Buck as he slept.

The first thing that caught his eye was the morning sun shimmering off the spilled bike's handlebars, not ten yards away. His eyes didn't want to focus, so he drifted off again for a few minutes, only to snort awake when a piece of trash blew against his face, tickling his nose. Buck felt the now-hard ground under him and the rocks that jutted into his aching side. He tried to jump to his feet but barely moved; a yelp of pain escaped his lips.

The next few moments were confusing. He was back in New York again, lying with his head against some curb, trying to sleep, trying to just keep breathing. Buck remembered how even the curbside got soft after a while. He would lie there, feigning a drugged stupor, so the gangs wouldn't kick his head in and kill him. He had gone to the city as a "noble savage," to show people who had never seen one what an Indian looked like; he'd left there months later just savage, bitter, and beaten. He had toyed with many identities through the years, thinking they were all facets of his Indian-ness, only to find out he was a con, a drifter, a fanatic, a preacher, a pusher who had dark skin and black eyes and just happened to look Indian.

It was noon now. He had to get up. Buck was stiff but not nearly as injured as he had at first feared. Though the gash across his forehead looked the worst, his shoulder hurt the most. Buck sat in the grass on the far side of the ditch for a while, just listening. He had been in the cities so much in the last ten years, he wasn't used to the quiet. The natural world he had assumed was a part of him, that he had gone into the cities to fiercely display, was no more a part of him than the wind was a part of the trees. The trees reflected the air rushing through their branches, whether that air was a delicate summer breeze or the gales of winter that bent them to the frozen ground. I'm like that, Buck thought, sitting there with his head in his hands. And right now I feel every storm that's ever hit me.

After a while, he became aware of the sound of water over rocks. Buck got shakily to his feet to look for the source of that sound. He walked a dozen yards back from the ditch, pushing through the underbrush. There he found a little rushing stream glinting in the sunlight, weaving its way through weeds and dense brush. Buck bent over the stream where it formed a clear pool and saw a stranger looking back at him.

It was an old warrior, one who had fought so hard against being helpless in a war-torn world that he himself had become the war. He could see the ravages of battle on him, the scarred and hardened shell that had all but obliterated what it had been erected to protect. Buck dropped to his knees and splashed handfuls of water over his face. He saw the wall of fear that sur-rounded him—he had been so afraid of being afraid. He had been terrified of complacently giving in, of letting the world crush his spirit into another little piece of its machinery.

Buck thought of his brother Bill, August really: August who had told them to call him Bill, August who had, inch by inch, Buck observed, bartered away his spirit to keep the peace. The last time Buck had visited Bill, a year ago, he had been aghast when he saw the war inside his brother. The quiet facade that encircled Bill's life was really the deadly stillness that precedes a huge funnel cloud.

Buck had tried to warn August about what he saw within him, but how could he tell his brother to beware of himself? August had replied, "Look, Buck, I see nothing but a dead end in what you're doing. Drugs, protests, jail. You're destroying any chance you have of getting it together."

"You mean I'm destroying any chance of 'fitting in' like you are. I guess I'm getting too close to the nice little deal you've got going with yourself, huh? Bye, Bill." Buck had taken off with a renewed vengeance to never sell out.

Now, drying his face on the front of his shirt, he wasn't so sure he hadn't given the enemy all his strength in the struggle. What did it matter if you sold out or were tricked into giving it away? In the end you were left with the same thing: nothing.

Buck walked back up to the road to look at his bike. One mirror had broken off and shattered, but otherwise it was func-tional. Groaning, he picked up the bike and dusted off the cracked seat. It was a big old Harley that he'd stolen four years earlier in Cincinnati. He knew how to keep it running, which was more than he could say for himself, right now.

Buck studied the skid marks on the narrow road and won-dered how it had happened. He was on a remote stretch of road going through the reservation. He could see Eagle Mountain in the distance, blue against the horizon. He loved it out here but he laughed in self-derision. He lived in the cities—he rode from city to city like the ghost of an ancient warrior, warning white settlers of the power of his kind. But there was no power, he now realized, when he never lived what he proclaimed was his life. He was too busy chasing the enemy to ever go home. It had started way back when he went to their schools and learned their ways. Buck had gotten so wrapped up in hating them that he had forgotten to nurture what he loved.

This last year had almost done him in. Buck met a girl, a woman really, who had a son of her own, eight years old. She was white, that's what he couldn't understand. She was older than Buck by three years and had no one but her son. Grace had told him right away she had no idea who Jock's father was. It had been too many years ago to even guess.

Grace lived on the edge of a very small town in the foothills of the Colorado Rockies, in an eight-foot-by-twenty-five-foot trailer, dominated by an old cast-iron woodstove; that was how Grace and Jock both kept warm and cooked.

"Why don't you go live in some larger town and get something to do?" Buck had asked her that first night.

"Why?" she'd asked back. "Not all us non-Indians want to live in town, you know. I wish I had a reservation to live on; I'd sit right in the middle of it and never come out."

Buck had felt the anger rise up in him when she'd said that. You stupid fool, he wanted to say, you'd wake up one morning and they'd have moved right on up to your doorstep. He'd kept his mouth shut though, because it was a long cold winter ahead. Buck knew that when the city got too hot, this would be the quietest place he'd have to come to.

Through that whole year, Grace had welcomed him whenever he showed up. She told him he was like a grizzly, a vanishing species, and she wanted to get a good look at him, before he was gone.

Jock liked him too. He'd been shy at first but had warmed up when Buck offered to take him into the mountains. On weekends, they would roam around together; Grace often came along too. Buck felt a stillness creeping inside him during those times, and then the panic.

"I gotta leave." He'd slammed down his fist on the wobbly table inside her trailer, breaking it. He grabbed his jacket, pulled on his boots, and roared away into the icy darkness. He'd gone a hundred miles through the night into the nearest large city, picked out the rowdiest-looking bar he could find, and drank until he wanted to tear up the place. He'd gotten his nose broken and one hand badly cut. But he'd shown them he could fight back. They wouldn't rob him of his life; he'd give it to them, drop by bloody drop.

He had spent the next month in jail, never missing the stillness of the mountains he could have gotten drunk on instead. If I could just break a few more heads, Buck had mused sitting in jail that month, I wouldn't mind my own busted-up life so much. He had given no thought to the stillness of the mountains.

Grace had come by near the end of the month to tell Buck she was leaving for California. She had also told him that she was going to have his baby. "I'm going to give the city a shot, like you said. Maybe I can get a decent job and a nice house to live in." Then Grace had turned away so he couldn't see her crying—but he had. Buck couldn't say a word. He'd nagged at her to go into town and "get it together;" now he wanted to shout, "Don't leave the mountains! If you go, who am I fighting to save them for?"

Grace and Jock had left, Jock looking back with big confused eyes as they had slipped out the visiting room door. Those eyes had haunted Buck the rest of his stay in jail. When he had got out, the first thing he had done was to go back to Grace's old trailer. It was still there, sagging, cold, and dilapidated against the evening sky, the mountains fading to silver in the background.

Buck hadn't been able to stop himself from looking in the cracked front window. He had half-expected to see Grace and Jock in there, a simmering pot on the old stove. But the trailer had been empty. It had been more than empty; it had ached with loneliness, with the sense that nobody was there to love it. Buck had wanted to scream and shatter the trailer with the ferocity of his anguish. For the first time, he had felt aware of the impotence of rage.

He could destroy the trailer, destroy all the reminders of where he and Grace had eaten meals, kept at bay the cold, made love. He could tear apart all the memories of talking to Jock, watching the mountains, looking up at the stars. He could roar and shatter the stillness of this place. But Buck had known, even before he had begun, that when he was done, the quiet would return to claim him.

Buck had sat down on a log by the front of the trailer and stared at the trees for some sign that he wasn't alone, some proof that fighting the enemy was the way to guarantee survival. But the forest had barely moved that night, and the few whispers through the trees that Buck had heard, he hadn't been able to understand. He had finally crawled inside the trailer through a broken back window, wrapped up in a faded quilt Grace had left, and waited for it to get light outside.

Buck must have dozed off because he had awakened the next morning thinking about August. For some reason he had felt he should see him, even though he knew their last visit had been tense and he'd left disappointed and angry. Buck had thought of Lottie and how the stillness around him now reminded him of her place. His place, his childhood home. He had gone to see Lottie a few times over the years, but had always bolted after a brief visit.

His mother's life, and his father's too, seemed passive to him. Buck didn't know what they should have done to stop the encroachment of the white world, but he had wanted them to do something. Instead, Amos had had a strange kind of power that moved him inward. Lottie followed suit, and now she was alone, living in a world that was all but invisible. Buck still believed that somehow the changes could be undone and reversed. He knew now that was what he had wanted all these years. Admitting that they couldn't be reversed was like dying.

Buck had felt the angry strength running out of him. But, rather than sinking down onto the ground right there outside the trailer, never to move again, he had experienced a strange lightness, like he had no body. He was on his bike and headed down the road before he had known what was happening.

He had ridden through that day and into the evening, not aware of when he had stopped for gas or to get a soda. By nightfall, he had almost reached the reservation, aware now of entering the silent, forested hills on that remote back road. It had been peaceful, and the peace had scared him. Buck was not used to being so alone with himself. Seeing the forces inside him, that were him, had made Buck break out into a sweat despite the cold night air blowing against his face.

Buck had swerved from side to side along the deserted road, feeling with panic the unseen enemy that pursued him. He had slid around the next curve vaguely aware that the bike was going down, too busy grappling with the dark force that squeezed him tightly around the middle. It had not wanted his body so much as his will to survive.

It had not gotten him yet. He was bruised, the gash on his head looked nasty, but he wasn't dead. His derisive laugh of a moment before sounded hollow in his ears. He had exhausted himself hating the enemy that was change, he thought suddenly, but he was damned if he was going to hate himself. If he turned to doing that, he knew it would get him. He'd disappear like the way of being he had desperately fought to defend. He'd been so busy fighting that he hadn't had time to live the way he was fighting for.

It all ran around in circles inside his head. Buck leaned the bike against a large tree and took a deep breath, then remounted and kicked it into sputtering life. The countryside shone bright and still, listening for his approach.

Buck rode the miles filled with a feeling of peace. The sunshine, the air, seemed charged with an expectancy. He watched Eagle Mountain loom closer all the time like an awesome giant, skirting the edge of it with the strange feeling that he was it; the clouds encasing the mountain's highest peak seemed to brush his ears. By midafternoon, he found a gas station not far from Lottie's, and a few miles from August's place in town. When he called August, he was sure he felt those high clouds chilling him. As he spoke to his brother, he felt his voice become tight and guarded again, erecting the defenses that had always protected him.

"I need a place to stay for tonight. I know you don't like me around, I blow your image. But look, I've had some bad luck, made some bad moves." Buck drew on the old armor and felt the old hatred. Only this time he realized it was destroying him, more than anything else.

"Come on over. I've blown my own image; I did it all by myself. It's probably the best thing I've ever done." August's response took him by surprise. He felt disarmed and strangely warmed.

"Yeah?" Buck felt a glimmer of hope as he shook the thing that was trying to grab him tight, off his back. "See ya in a while."

He kicked the bike back into action again and headed the few miles over to August's house. He passed the turnoff to Lottie's place and noted that the old log cabin peeked through the trees at the new world across the road. The development sat impassive yet relentless, as does all change. For once, Buck didn't race through in defiance of the speed limit, but he couldn't help gunning the bike a little towards the end, like a dog lifting his leg just once more on his neighbor's turf. Buck grinned to himself. He reached inside his pocket for his sunglasses and felt the slip of paper he'd picked up at Grace's trailer.

She'd left the address where she was in California on top of the quilt he'd wrapped himself in that night. How did she know? How did he know he'd be able to find her in the city? Right now, he was on his way to his brother's. If he could find his way back to August, back to himself, maybe he could find his way back to a lot of things.

Epilogue

August and Buck half-dragged, half-slid the long sofa through the hall and up against the varnished front door. Buck straightened up, rubbing his sore left side. It had been three months since he'd laid his Harley down on the pavement and woken up in a ditch, and his side still bothered him some.

"Hurt much?" August wiped his hand across his own sweaty forehead as he looked over at his brother.

"Nah. Just stiffens up sometimes. Reminds me I'm still human, even if I am an enlightened Indian." Buck's playful arrogance brought a smile to August's normally serious face. It was good to see his twin brother's humor again.

During their early years in school, Buck's humor had often lightened many an otherwise-gloomy situation. To the two brothers, the "white people" attitudes seemed to make for a joyless existence, having to buy everything: land, animals, people, respectability, even the right to have fun. August was the one who wanted to scream with a white rage back then.

Buck had poked fun at the whole situation of being enraged and of being white. He had mimicked their speech and, with a deadpan expression, asked for August's I.D., his right to be here. All the kids at the bus stop would end up laughing as Buck would go around asking all of them for proof that they were supposed to be here, on the bus.

When they got on the bus, he'd threaten to throw them off and forbid them to go to school, since "they weren't legal." Then the kids would whoop and holler "Great, great, let's ditch. Let's

49

run away!" Buck would grab their arms and tickle them, saying, "No you don't. You don't have the right to do that! We own all the land. Where would you run to?" He'd gotten innumerable "tickets" from the bus drivers through the years for being so disruptive. Buck had thrown them away with a smile, and everything had gotten more out of hand. The bus driver would glare down at Buck, while Buck would stand there looking back defiantly. No bus driver had actually kicked Buck off the bus because they all knew that's what he wanted.

August had watched the white world's reaction to Buck out of the corner of his eye and learned something. Since he knew he couldn't be accepted with the "white rage" he was feeling, he smiled a lot and decided to just keep the "white" part of it. Somewhere down the line, the brothers had changed places. August had stifled his anger and become pleasantly numb, while Buck had lost all humor and never laughed at anything.

We definitely are two sides of the same thing, August had often thought back then, when he mused on the difference between himself and Buck. He thought that now as he glanced at his brother, but realized also that they had many feelings, which blended into the oneness of who they were.

Buck was staying with August and his family in town, had been for the last three months since his accident. The two brothers had reached a common ground of tolerance, not just for themselves and their world, but the world beyond. Buck's hatred and rage had almost killed him, as had August's denial that he even was angry.

"You really wanna get rid of all this stuff, August?" Buck looked over at the stacks of furniture, clothing, toys, and basement odds-and-ends out in the driveway. "I could use some of it when I move out."

"Help yourself, but I don't know where you're going to put it. I've got to lighten up our load. I don't know when we're moving, or where, but it's going to be smaller and simpler from now on. I've outgrown all this, you might say," August added with an airy wave of his hand. "Let's load it up and get to the dump," he went on. "Bernard wants his truck back by tonight." They had borrowed their brother's beat-up junker for the day.

Buck sorted through and kept a few things: some old jeans, two chairs, and a couple of blankets. He turned around to tell his brother he was ready and saw August huffing out the front door with an armload of brown canvas.

"The old tent," August gasped. "It's large and heavy, ten-foot-by-fourteen-foot. You could set it up out in the hills somewhere if you want and store your stuff in it."

"Store my stuff? Hell. I'll live in it!" Buck helped August squash it down in the corner of Bernard's truck, along with the few other items he was keeping.

They arrived at the dump just as a new four-wheel-drive pickup turned down the dusty side road to the county landfill.

"Nice truck," Buck commented, as he pulled in behind and followed it down.

August looked over at Buck with a funny expression. "You haven't seen Rosemary since you've been back this time, have you?"

"Nah. I will one of these days. But you know, I'm still sorting things out, and she's, well, real civilized, you might say." Buck glanced back at his brother.

"You always thought I was real civilized, too," August shot back.

"Yeah, but you're changing. Look at all this junk you're unloading. You'd think you were the old man, with all his dislike of modern stuff. Hey, why'd you ask about Rosemary anyhow?" Buck watched the truck ahead pull over and started to go around.

"That's her. Her and Ed got that truck a few months ago." August looked over again for his brother's reaction.

"Shit! Why didn't you say so!" Buck slammed on the brakes and jumped out next to the new vehicle that didn't look like it drove off-road very much. The tires were still clean.

"Rosemary, hey, hi!" Buck bounded over to the side of the shiny, red-and-white vehicle. He put his hand on the door as Rosemary rolled down the tinted window.

"Buck, how are you?" Rosemary looked good, if white, Buck found himself thinking, making note of her tight western shirt tucked into the stiff jeans. Oh, cut it out, he snapped to himself, you haven't seen her in ages.

"I'm okay. I've been staying over at August's, uh Bill's, for the last couple months. I had an accident, and. . ." He could feel Rosemary tighten up, nervous about her crazy brother. He could feel his defenses ready to spring up, too. Normally, this was the point at which he would start getting angry and tense and begin his assault on her way of being. But he'd been doing too much thinking about his own way of being lately, and though he felt alone and vulnerable without his anger, Buck stood his ground. As it frequently had of late, the struggle turned inward, and his old targets lost their appeal.

"Hey, Rosemary, let me and August" (that's what he'd call him now, even if Rosemary preferred the more conventional Bill) "help you unload. August's been cleaning house, too."

August watched his brother from behind, from inside Bernard's truck, and was glad to see Buck's shoulders relax. It made him feel vulnerable himself to notice how naked and unprotected Buck looked.

"Thanks, sure, Buck. I've only got a few sacks of trash and an old piece of carpet we used in the workroom. It's just my weekly dump run."

Buck and August silently lifted the black trash bags over the side of the truck. One caught on a sharp piece of metal and ripped open. Papers and cartons and all kinds of plastic wraps and containers spilled out over the ground. Jesus, that's a lot of stuff for one week, Buck thought. It fits right in with all this other garbage from the land of plenty, he couldn't help noticing.

Waste dump, that's what they call it. There's a lot of waste, all right. He was suddenly back criss-crossing the country on his bike again, seeing the ravaged hills and torn land. And the trees. His name was One Tree, and he hoped he wasn't the only thing left called tree in twenty years. He felt an urge to touch and know the earth while he still could, though he himself had used enough of those comforts that came in the cartons and plastic that blew across the open land now. August was next to him lifting the shaggy blue carpet out of Rosemary's truck.

"Hey, Rosemary, I could use this. I'm gonna set up August's old tent in the woods somewhere for awhile." Buck lifted the carpet from August's arms.

"Sure, Buck, take it." Rosemary smiled hesitantly and for the first time, looked directly at her brother.

August, noticing the change, ventured to speak. "After Buck and I finish dumping this junk of mine, why don't you follow us over to Lottie's. We've got to take Bernard's truck back and get my car. It's been a long time since we were all there together."

"You don't have to be polite, Bill. . .I mean, August," Rosemary stammered. "I've been afraid of being sucked back into a place that doesn't exist anymore. Isn't that crazy? I miss it sometimes, and I miss being together with all of you, but I've worked hard to get where I am and I love it!" She spoke loudly now, looking right in Buck's face.

"Hey, Rosie, haven't we all? I nearly killed myself getting here." Buck's old humor was surfacing, but he was strangely serious, too.

"I'll follow you," Rosemary said, climbing back into her truck.

Lottie was sitting on the weathered plank bench outside her cabin when they all pulled up. Bernard, a taller version of his older brothers, slammed out the screen door with a beer in one hand when he heard the trucks drive into the yard. Lottie looked from one to the other and smiled broadly, getting up from her spot.

"You're all here just in time for dinner," Lottie hummed, as if she'd planned it all. She always seems to know what's going on before we do, August thought to himself.

Over dinner Buck talked about where he planned to set up the tent. It was a spot over behind the forested rise in back of Lottie's cabin and almost two miles down an obscure dirt trail that led into a little hidden valley, he said. Bernard offered to help him set things up, "long as I can stay out there sometimes," he added.

"Unless I want to be out there alone, you're more than welcome," Buck grinned back.

"I want to come out and see it," Rosemary spoke up, walking over to the old woodburner to get herself another warm tortilla. She turned to go sit down again and was surprised to see her brothers all staring at her. "Well, I do. Even if I wouldn't want to stay out there," she continued, coloring. She was embarrassed and embraced by a warmth at the same time. "Edward will envy you, Buck, being out like that," Rosemary went on, still feeling exposed.

"He could do it, too," Buck heard himself saying. He realized Ed could if he wanted. "Hell, anyone could," Buck said out loud. "You just have to want to learn how."

Lottie got up, scraping together all the leftovers from their plates. There wasn't much, so she added a few heaping spoonfuls from the pot on the stove. "For the coyote," she smiled, nodding to her family.

"I thought you had to sneak out and put it down when he couldn't see you do it." Rosemary watched Lottie get ready to go outside. The coyote had been hanging back by the edge of the trees the whole time they were eating dinner. Sometimes he even hopped out into plain sight, standing there waving his moth-eaten tail before ducking into the trees again. They had been surprised at how bold he was with them all here.

"Oh, no. Sometimes, now, he lets me get as close to him as from the cabin to the clothesline. He just stands there watching me until I put the plate down. Then he trots in a circle around me until I leave and he can eat." Lottie pushed open the back door and started up towards the treeline.

The coyote stayed hidden until she was well away from the house. He then ran-hopped across the bare ground towards Lottie with surprising speed. Lottie stopped, holding the dish of food against her. August, Buck, Rosemary, and Bernard could see her through the window, a dark figure against the evening sky, dwarfed by Eagle Mountain in the background. They could feel her holding as still as the mountain, barely breathing, wondering if the coyote would come any closer this evening.

The coyote stopped abruptly in his three-legged charge and became a black silhouette creeping in tense silence nearer and nearer; soon his nose was only a few inches from Lottie's long wool skirt. For what seemed an eternity, he stayed like that, not moving, not twitching an ear or tail. Then he pulled back his old, grey lips and nipped lightly at her skirt, giving it a small tug. Lottie looked him directly in the eye and gave an imperceptible nod of her head. Then she bent over and put the food down; as soon as she moved the coyote seemed to fly backward through the air. Lottie turned and walked back to the house.

"Mama, I can't believe that!" Rosemary grabbed Lottie as she came through the door. "Do you think he'll ever let you touch him?" Rosemary was asking for all of them, Lottie knew, looking at all their startled faces.

"Oh, I don't know, Rosie," she answered, using her daughter's old childhood name. Her voice was filled with affection for her daughter, her three sons, and the old coyote. "I may have to wait until *I'm* an old coyote to do that!"

LOTTIE'S SONG

Are you going out in the night
To become one of the stars?
Remember though you may travel there,
You'll be Here, wherever you are.

Are you going up on the hill
To become the wandering wind?
Remember though you may travel far,
You'll be Here, beginning to end.

Are you going down that dusty road,
Through the noise, confusion and smog?
Remember when the sun shines again,
You'll be able to see very far.
Yes, you'll be able to see very far.

Author's Biography

ANNETTE R. SCHOBER (Grace Deer) lives in the mountains of central Arizona. Her father was French-Canadian Indian, and this background has given her a deep reverence for the earth and nature. She lives simply in a mountain home at the end of many miles of dirt road, without electricity, running water, or television.

"This is not a fad lifestyle taken up on a whim," Ms. Schober says, "but a chosen way of being. I feel very grateful for the opportunity to be a woman of the earth."

She began writing poetry and short stories when she was eleven years old and has had her poetry published. In 1989, she received an award in the nationwide Phoenix Poetry Society annual competition for her poem "Yesterday."

Ms. Schober likes to roam the hills and feel the spirit. She has a husband, a child, and many dogs who sometimes accompany her.